For Jill and Semadar,
who always manage to figure out
what I'm trying to say.

Philomel Books

Published by the Penguin Group | Penguin Group (USA) LLC
375 Hudson Street, New York, NY 10014

USA | Canada | UK | Ireland | Australia | New Zealand | India | South Africa | China
penguin.com | A Penguin Random House Company

Library of Congress Cataloging-in-Publication Data is available upon request.

Manufactured in China | ISBN 978-0-399-16606-8 | 10 9 8 7 6 5 4 3 2 1

Edited by Jill Santopolo | Design by Semadar Megged | Text set in Kidprint MT Std.
The art was created with traditional media and Photoshop.

BAH! Said the Baby

Jennifer Plecas

Philomel Books
An Imprint of Penguin Group (USA)

BAH! said the Baby.

"The Baby said 'bah!'"
Mom cried.
"What is it, Baby? Book?
Do you want my book,
Baby?"

"Ball!" said Brother. "I think Baby wants the ball!"

"Bow?" said Sister. "Does Baby want to touch my bow?"

"The Baby said 'bah!'"
Brother cried.

"What is it, Baby? Brother?
Do you want your brother,
Baby?"

"Maybe Baby wants
the bunny," said Sister.
"The lamb says 'baa,'"
said Mom. "Do you want
your lamb, Baby?"

BAH!

said the Baby.

"The Baby said 'bah!'"
Sister cried.
"What is it, Baby? Bear?
Do you want the bear?"

"Block?" said Brother.
"Bottle?" said Mom. "Do
you want your bottle, Baby?"

"Bah-bah?" said Sister.

"Bah-bah?" said Brother.

"BYE-BYE!" said Mom.

"The Baby said 'BYE-BYE!'"

"Bye-bye, Baby!" said Mom.
"Bye-bye, Baby!" said Brother.
"Bye-bye, Baby!" said Sister.

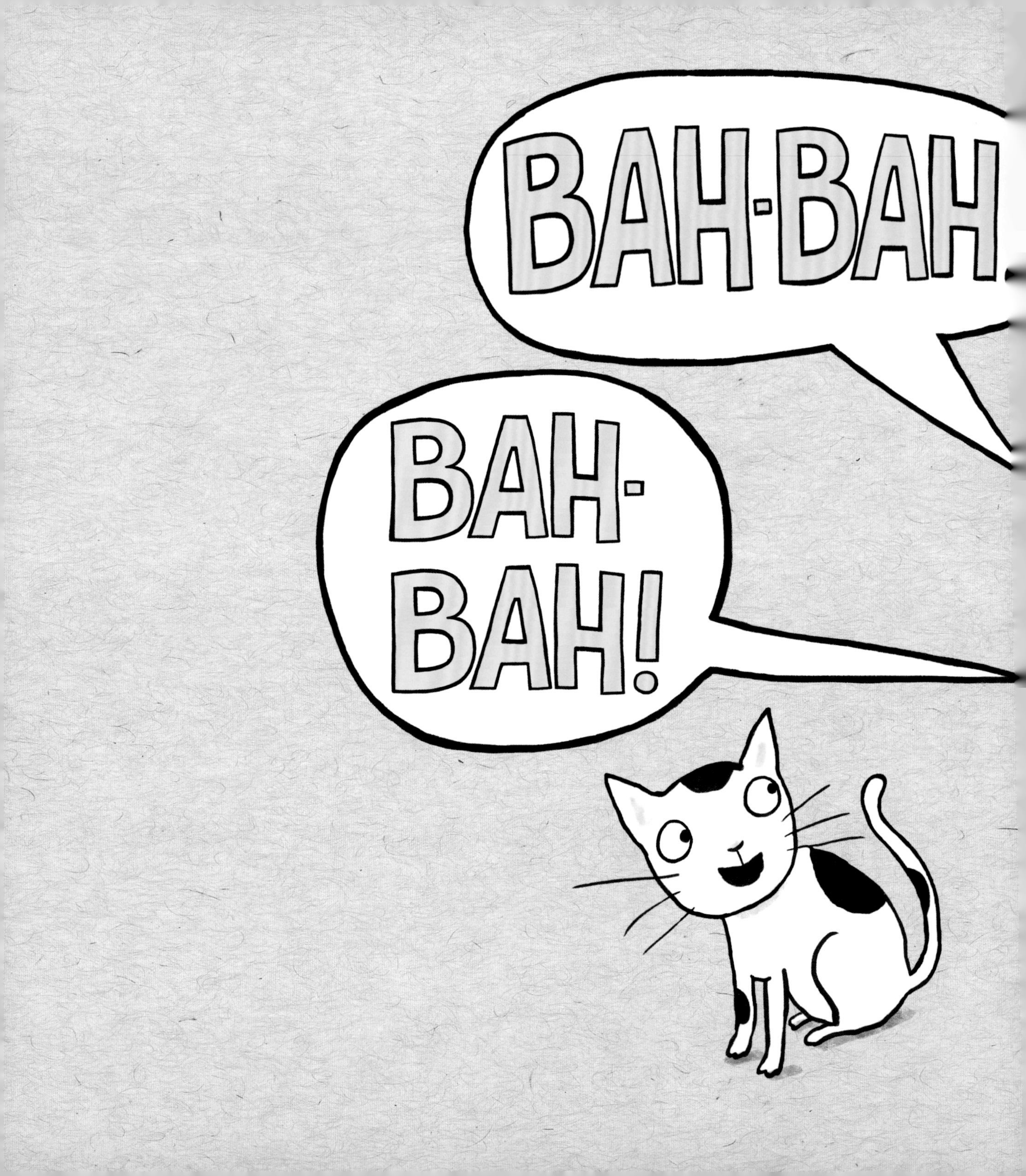
BAH-BAH
BAH-BAH!

said the Baby.

"Hello, Baby!" said Sister.
"Hello, Baby," said Brother.
"Hello, Baby!" said Mom.

"Can you say 'hello,' Baby?" said Mom.
"Say 'hello,' Baby!" said Brother.
"Hello, Baby!" said Sister.